For Freedom

Written By, Michele Snyder

Illustrated By, Amy Cappelli

To

Tyler, Rudy and Chan,

You are the inspiration for this story.

To

The men and women who sacrifice so much to serve and protect this country and those in need,

All in the name of Freedom.

It was what Tyler thought would be a typical start to a new school year. His family had just moved from the West Coast to the East Coast. Tyler wasn't new to the community. He had lived there a few years before, but most of the faces had changed.

Tyler moved back just in time for the new school year to start. He did not have much time to make many new friends. He certainly missed his old friends, but was looking forward to making many new ones.

School started just like any other year, just as Tyler had thought it would. Each classroom brought in a new teacher. Each teacher spent the entire class time going over what was expected from the students for the school year.

Lunch came and recess went. Just when Tyler thought he couldn't take one more first day lecture, Miss Nelson introduced herself to the class and caught his attention. She was the Writing teacher and already had a very special assignment for them.

Most of the class moaned, knowing with the assignment their summer break had come to an end. Not Tyler, he listened with great interest to every word she had to say. Miss Nelson had assigned the class to write an essay, not the traditional "How I Spent My Summer," but instead, an essay on what one parent does for a living.

As Tyler began to write his essay, he thought long and hard, remembering all of the times he and his Dad spent together discussing the very same thing. Tyler was really trying to put into words all of the things his Dad had shared with him about his job and who he worked for. Finally, he came up with just the right ones.

The day came for the class to share their essays. It was Tyler's turn and he began to share... "My Dad's work can call him away from home. He may be gone a short time and sometimes he will be gone a long while. He works in all types of conditions and works with many others just like him".

My Dad's work helps us feel safe so we can ride our bikes down the street, or play our favorite games with our friends.

My Dad's work gives us the Freedom to watch cartoons on Saturday mornings and our favorite shows at night.

My Dad works for our right to read our favorite books and fun magazines.

Thanks to my Dad's work, we can wear whatever kind of clothes we want.

Because of my Dad's work, we can go to any type of church and believe in any kind of faith we wish.

My Dad's work lets us eat dinners with our families and sleep safely in our warm beds.

You see, My Dad works for Freedom and he helps make sure we can grow up to be whatever we want to be.

Tyler was proud of his essay, but most of all he was proud of his Dad. He knew his Dad had a difficult job and couldn't always be with him, but Tyler also knew because of this...

he would always be Free!

Love & Thanks to

My loving husband and wonderful family, I couldn't have done it without you!

JoJo, You do know best!

Amy Cappelli & Shonda Lewis, I have enjoyed the adventure!

All of the For Freedom Supporters & Proud Americans!

Copyright © 2006 by Michele Snyder
DreamCastle Publishing Office
Publishing Office
6215 Hickory Lawn Court
Grove City, OH 43123
ISBN 0-9778663-0-0
SAN: 850-3664
Printed in the United States of America.